CW00847740

Billy Boggle and the Melted Vegetables

Jen Selinsky

Illustrated by

Teresa Amehana Garcia

Published by Pen It! Publications, LLC in the U.S.A.
812-371-4128   www.penitpublications.com

ISBN: 978-1-63984-029-8

Illustrated by Teresa Amehana Garcia

Billy Boggle came home from school one day and opened the refrigerator door.

But when he grabbed the bag of carrots, it was all gooey and wet inside.

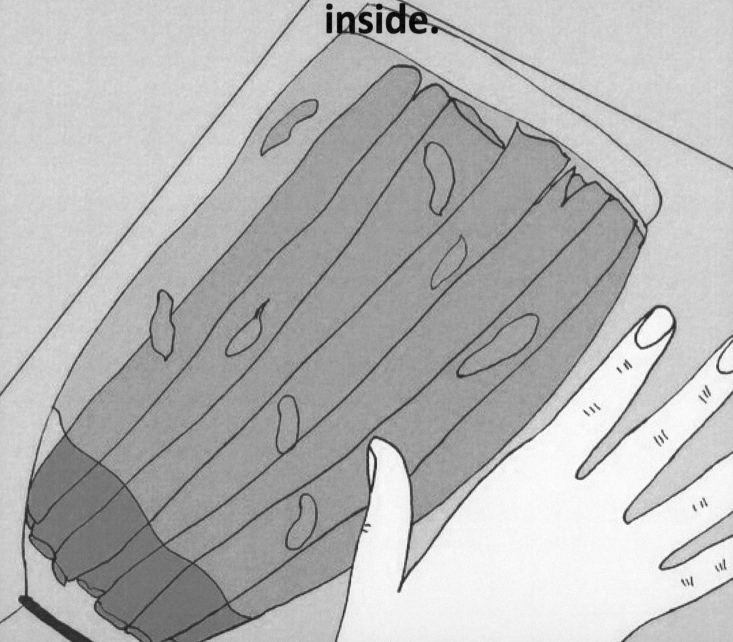

Then, he reached for some celery, and what was inside that bag was melted green.

"Mom!" he yelled.
"What happened to all the vegetables?"

As soon as Mrs. Boggle came into the kitchen, she saw the leaky bags of orange and green. "Yuk! What a mess. Billy, please help me clean this up before it gets all over the counter."

They poured the gooey vegetables into the sink, threw away the bags, and wiped off the counter.

Billy put his finger to his chin and thought for a moment.

Was something wrong with their refrigerator? Did they keep the food in there for too long?

Billy's mom went into the living room and turned the TV on. The news lady talked about how vegetables all over the world were melting, and even the top scientists couldn't figure out why.
What was going on?

Billy went back to his room
and got dressed.
Today, he was going to his
best friend, Jerry's, house.

Once his mom dropped him off there, Billy got out of the car and knocked on the door.

Jerry's mom led him into the kitchen, where Jerry was.

Billy's jaw dropped when he walked into the room. There were piles of liquid everywhere, on the counters, on the floor, and even on the table.

Jerry had on his white jacket and safety goggles. "Hello, Billy," he said when he saw his friend.

"Why are there colors of liquid puddles everywhere?"

"I'm trying to figure out what turned the vegetables into liquid, but I haven't had any success so far."

"Want me to help?" Billy asked.

"Sure," Jerry said. "Maybe we can discover something if we put our heads together."

Both boys were puzzled until Billy spied the blender on the far counter.

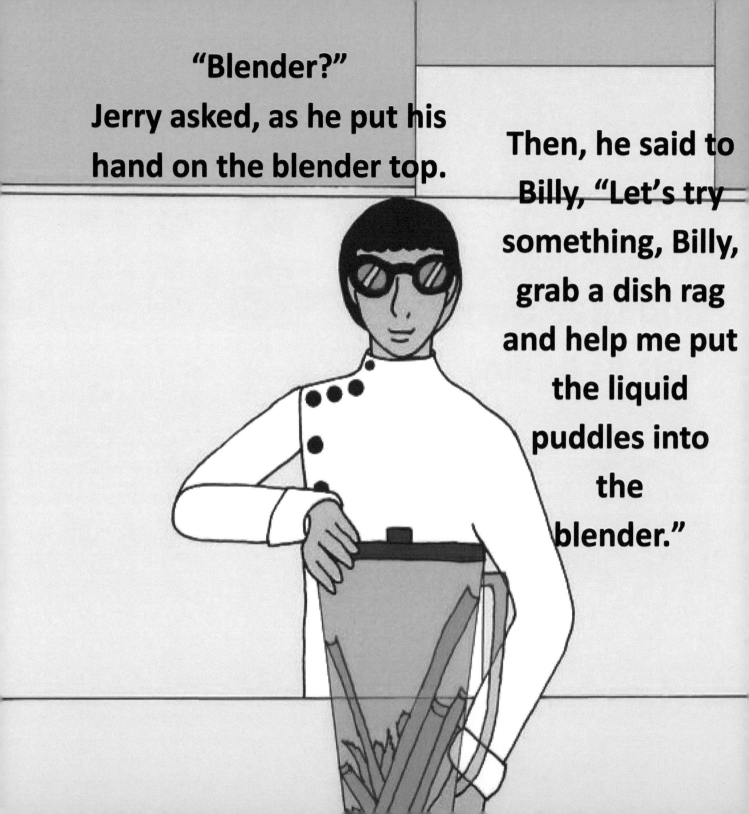

Billy did what his friend suggested.

Once they filled the blender, Jerry put on the lid and turned it on. After only a few seconds, the vegetables became solid again. Billy smiled.

"Billy, you're a genius!" Jerry said before he took a piece of celery out of the blender.

He took a bite. "This tastes great! Try one, Billy!"

Billy took a bite of a carrot.

It did not take long for the news to spread, and everyone all over the world made their vegetables come back to normal.

When Billy got home that night, his mom made the whole family the roast beef and vegetable medley.

The End